For my son, the Herbie-saurus. G.P.J.

For my son, the Codie-opteryx. G.P.

American edition published in 2015 by Andersen Press USA, an imprint of Andersen Press Ltd.
www.andersenpressusa.com

First published in Great Britain in 2014 by Andersen Press Ltd..
20 Vauxhall Bridge Road, London SW1V 2SA.

Published in Australia by Random House Australia Pty.,
Level 3, 100 Pacific Highway, North Sydney, NSW 2060.

Text copyright © Gareth P. Jones, 2014.

Illustration copyright © Gary Parsons, 2014.

Distributed in the United States and Canada by
Lerner Publishing Group, Inc.
241 First Avenue North
Minneapolis, MN 55401 USA

For reading levels and more information,
look up this title at www.lernerbooks.com.

Color separated in Switzerland by Photolitho AG, Zürich.

Printed and bound in Malaysia by Tien Wah Press.

Library of Congress Cataloging-in-Publication data available.

ISBN: 978-1-4677-6313-4

eBook ISBN: 978-1-4677-6317-2

1 - TWP - 07/1/14

The DINOSAURS are HAVING a PARTY!

Gareth P. Jones

Garry Parsons

ANDERSEN PRESS USA

The dinosaurs are having a party.

It starts precisely at three.

But I'm a boy not a dinosaur,

So I'm pleased they've invited me.

The dinosaurs are having a party.

It isn't too far on the bus.

The house is **vibrating** and **shaking**

But the neighbors aren't making a fuss.

A **big** dinosaur **appears** by the **door.**

He **smiles** and says "**Hello.**"

"There are **plenty** of **meat eaters** in here.
Are you **sure** you want to go?"

The dinosaurs are having a party.

Some are extremely tall.

Others inside are terribly wide.

So I SQUEEZE my way through the hall.

Stepping inside one of the rooms,

There's a game of musical chairs.

A little one loses and wails,

"Not fair! Nobody cares!"

So they change instead to musical **bumps**

The music suddenly stops.

The little one looks like he's winning . . .

Till he's **squished** by a **triceratops.**

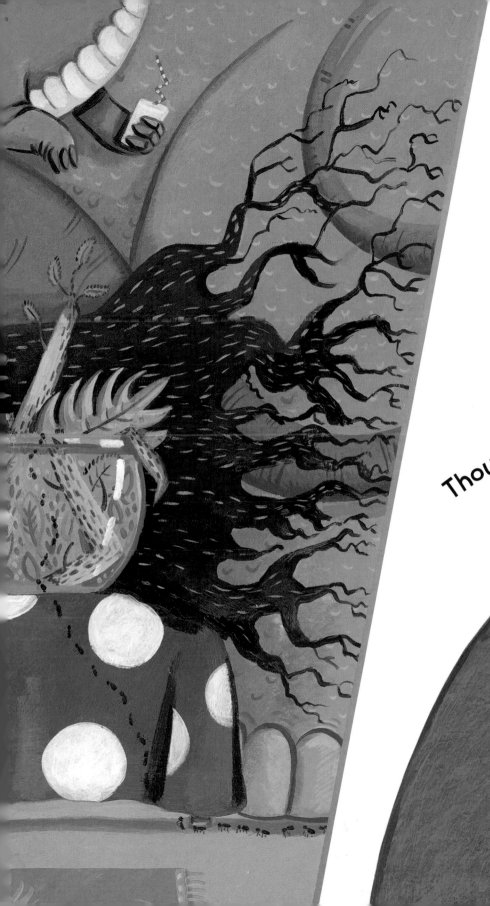

The dinosaurs are having a party.

There's plenty of food to gobble.

There are Jell-Os of every flavor.

Though **something** is making them **wobble.**

There's a barbecue in the back garden,
Though I can't see a morsel of meat.

The cook suggests I sit down,
But I don't like the look of the seat.

The bouncy castle is lots of fun,
For the whole of the dinosaur gang,
Until a **huge** stegosaurus **jumps** on

And **bursts** the **whole thing** with a **BANG!**

There's a really long line for the toilet.

Someone is being too slow.

One desperate dinosaur's shouting,

"Hurry up. We all need to go!"

Someone is flushing the toilet,
Then slowly pushing the door.
A **terrible** stink **spills** out,

Then . . .

T-Rex steps out with a

Roar!

I go to grab a party bag.
I've had such a lot of fun.

But T-Rex spots
me sneaking out.

So I break into a RUN.

I run

and run
and

run some more.

I only just catch the bus.
The driver shouts,

"Hold tight, everyone.

The **T-Rex** is **after us.**"

The driver turns left,

then right,
then left

Trying his best
to confuse him.

He goes round
and round
in circles . . .

Hurrah! We finally lose him!

I mostly enjoyed the dinosaurs' party.

There is just one little snag.

I don't think the bag I picked up . . .

Was really a **PARTY BAG!**